W9-CAI-304

For my father (N. P.)

If My Moon Was Your Sun

Andreas Steinhöfel
With Illustrations By Nele Palmtag

Translation by Matthew O. Anderson

Plough Publishing House

Published by Plough Publishing House
Walden, New York
Robertsbridge, England
Elsmore, Australia
www.plough.com

First published in Germany under the title *Wenn mein Mond deine Sonne wäre,*
copyright © 2015 by Carlsen Verlag GmbH, Hamburg, Germany
Musical recordings copyright © 2015 by SWR Media Services GmbH.

ISBN: 978-0-87486-079-5
22 21 20 19 18 17   1 2 3 4 5 6 7 8 9

Library of Congress Cataloging-in-Publication Data pending.
If My Moon Was Your Sun
Library of Congress Cataloging in Publication Control Number: 2017023106

Printed in Mexico

This is the story of Max, the one you read about in the newspapers or saw on TV. Do you remember? No? Max lives in a small town – one much smaller than yours. A few hills rise up around this town, all of them covered in trees. Between the highest hills runs a brook, which is followed on one side by a stony path with patches of dry grass – haven't you seen the pictures? What perfect summer scenes they were. You can imagine how they hurried along this path, Max and his grandfather, followed by Miss Schneider: three little hasty human dots whizzing by. Why were they in such a hurry? Well, you see, because they were running away. Because everyone was chasing them. Because that was the day Max kidnapped his grandfather. . . .

(2)   A Summer Day - Morning (Prokofiev)

Early one morning – just a week after his ninth birthday –
Max woke up filled with a feeling that something was
missing. The feeling tugged and tore at him, it was
endlessly deep and glowing, and it burned him from
inside.

A long time ago, while searching for that place where
our feelings of longing live, some people believed that
they had discovered the spot. Longing, they claimed,
lives in the heart. But Max knew better: his body was
made up of billions of tiny cells, and, since each one of
these cells hurt, it could only mean that his feeling of
longing lived *everywhere* in him. And, what's more, if his
soul was also made up of cells, then his longing filled

each of them too, because it flooded through every part
of him. No heart by itself could ever have enough room
for so much longing.

And so on this morning Max climbed out of bed – long
before his mother was awake. He brushed his teeth,
dressed, and packed his backpack in the kitchen with
care; and only after he had passed halfway through the
still-sleeping city – when the sun stood just above the
houses and kissed the crests of the rooftops – only then
did he realize what was driving him to put one foot in
front of the other so quickly and decisively.

Max grinned and walked a bit faster.

(4)   A Summer Day – Baseball (Prokofiev)

When Max opened the door to the nursing home, he was met with a muted, buzzing noise, the kind a beehive makes. He had been coming here for almost a year now, and that's how he knew that many of the old folks woke up early after a short night; they didn't need much sleep anymore. Most times, like now, a few of them sat together in the big common room reading the newspaper or playing cards or Parcheesi. Others shuffled between the tables or stood in the surrounding area with wrinkled foreheads and slight, quizzical smiles on

their faces that looked the same as they had the week before, and would look next week too. "They've lost their marbles," Grandfather had decided during Max's first visit. With a knowing wink, he had added, "Just like me!"

Actually, a year ago, grandfather still had nearly all his marbles. But his mind, as Mama had explained, was unfortunately functioning less and less well. Soon it wouldn't be enough for them to stop in at Grandfather's house now and then, as she and Max did. He would need someone to look after him all the time.

"Can't I do that?" Max had asked.

"When – during recess at school?" Mama had bit her lip. "I'm sorry, dear. I know that you're very attached to your grandfather, but it's not like he'll be gone forever if he moves into a place like this."

No, thought Max, as the door silently closed behind him, *not gone forever.* But he would be far away on the other side of town in a house full of old people who lived there as though trapped in a cage. The doors could only be opened from the inside if one of the staff typed a number code into the keypad on the wall. None of the nursing home residents knew this code.

Max tried to act as he always did in the nursing home: quiet, calm, and well, *Max-ish.* The few old faces that had quickly looked up when he came in were already looking down again. He nodded to Leon, the caregiver who had let him in. Leon smiled back briefly before he disappeared in a hurry down the next hallway. Everyone here knew Max.

He took a deep breath. It smelled like weak tea – peppermint and chamomile. The common room, with its warm yellow walls and windows that reached all the way down to the floor, was the exact opposite of the schoolyard with its hubbub and commotion. In here, quiet and warmth were the order of the day, and no loud words were ever spoken. For just a moment, Max felt comfortable and drowsy – the atmosphere of the nursing home surrounded him like a soft, protective blanket. For just a moment, he thought that what he'd like most was to breathe out slowly and stay here forever.

(6)   A Summer Day – Waltz (Prokofiev)

"Is the sun shining out there?"

A chirping sound. Max stared at the woman who was now blocking his path. Her spindly body was strangely crooked as though it had been cobbled together out of rough-sawn boards. From beneath a spider web of hair, her haggard face examined him closely. He tried remembering who she was – yes, this was Miss Schneider. When she was younger she had been . . . what exactly? His grandfather had told him, but Max couldn't remember. A teacher! Yes, a teacher of . . . something or other.

"Look out the window and you'll see for yourself," he said.

"The window on the left or the right?"

"Both, and the one in the middle too. Now, can I get past?"

Miss Schneider smiled as though he had just handed in an exam that, but for a tiny detail, would have earned a perfect score. But she didn't seem to plan on getting out of the way. Max pressed his lips together, hard. As if to say, *well, if you won't move, then neither will I.*

Still smiling, Miss Schneider stepped aside.

"Oh boy, oh boy! Oh boy, oh boy, oh boy!"

Three more "oh boys" later, Max stood before the door to his grandfather's room. He knocked and – without waiting for a response – turned the knob . . . and as the door opened, I want to tell you *why* Max felt the way he did, *why* he loved his grandfather so much. If you had asked Max yourself . . . well, he probably would have fumbled about for the right words. In the end he would have blurted out something like this: "Because he loves *me* so very much." And if you had replied, "Wow, Max, what a great explanation," only then, perhaps, would he have told you (and this was just one of many exam- ples) how it felt to sit in the garden – surrounded by the

sweet smell of autumn – and rest his tired head in Grandfather's lap after they had picked apples, and to feel the
great, heavy hands that lay so gently on his head. And
throughout all of this Max had listened to his grandfather humming – a sound you could only just hear, a
sound that always seemed to be rising from him. Max
had never been near his grandfather without hearing
this gentle humming, and when he had asked what it
was, this humming that softly and tenderly wove its way
through air and light, Grandfather would say the names
of famous composers: Brahms, Schubert, Mozart.

One of the two windows in Grandfather's room was crooked. You could open it enough to let in a little air, but not all the way. Grandfather sat fully dressed – *looking sharp,* as he himself would have said – at a small table, bent over the newspaper. He seemed to be having one of his better days. When Max entered the room, a bushy eyebrow shot upward questioningly.

"Who are you?"

"Santa Claus," said Max.

"Nonsense," snorted Grandfather. "You're my grandson."

"Max."

"That's right." He peered over Max's shoulder. "Where's your mother?"

"Work."

"Father?"

"Flew the coop."

"Ah, yes, right. And too bad for the chickens." Grandfather set the newspaper down in front of him. "What are you doing here so early?"

"Picking you up," answered Max. "We're getting out of here."

"Oh, we are, are we?"

If I close my eyes now, thought Max, *I can smell apples. And then I'll start to cry.*

He reached out a hand.

Grandfather began to hum.

(8)   A Summer Day – Regret (Prokofiev)

Grandfather's move into the nursing home last year had been a tedious to and fro, a never-ending in-again-and-out-again with crates, cases, and cardboard boxes; not to mention the furniture. As Max had stood waiting for the umpteenth time for the coded security door to open, a caregiver had quietly taken him aside and pointed to the numeric keypad by the door. "Here, try typing a big X."

So Max had pushed the keys from the upper left to the lower right – 1 5 9 – then from the upper right to the lower left – 3 5 7 – and strained to hold his breath as the door sprang open with a gentle whir.

"Keep that to yourself," the caregiver had made him promise. "OK?"

Max had nodded and kept the secret to himself. But whenever he had come to visit his grandfather in the following months, he had tested the code to see if it still worked. It did. Apparently they never changed it.

The big X worked today too. As Max steered Grandfather quickly through the entrance hall – all the while keeping an eye out in every direction in case one of the staff spotted them – he felt an almost painful tingling in his fingertips, which didn't go away until they could type that familiar X, 1 5 9, 3 5 7. After that, the whirring noise, a gust of fresh air, and three, four steps later: freedom.

Afterward, Max couldn't have told you for all the money in the world whether Miss Schneider had slipped out ahead of, behind, or beside them as he and his grandfather emerged from the home.

"Toward the sun?" asked Miss Schneider.

"Toward the bus stop," said Max. "Keep it snappy."

(10) A Summer Day - March (Prokofiev)

Never in the history of escapes has there been a more laid-back getaway than that of Max, his grandfather, and Miss Schneider – aside from the zig-zagging route they took to the bus stop. The mostly empty bus that brought them out of town seemed to glide rather than drive through the summer morning. At some point the city limit sign whizzed past. Fields and meadows lay stretched out before them now, a green glow with red, yellow, and blue spots here and there; and further off: the hills. Max squeezed his grandfather's hand and grinned up at him.

"Do you know where we're going?"

"I bet I do," replied his grandfather.

"Are you glad?"

A buzzing sound answered him, or maybe it was a hum. From above the back of the front seat, bony fingers were twisting a handful of spiderweb-gray hair into a little bun. Max leaned back in his seat, content. It could take a long time – with a bit of luck until lunchtime – before anyone in the home noticed that two of the residents were missing. Leon would then remember that Max had been there early that morning, and realize that the grandson might have possibly somehow . . .

And that's when the fun really begins, thought Max. A grin stole onto his face. Probably they would call the police. There would be announcements on the radio. Search parties would scour the streets in all directions, until someone would think to call and ask the bus lines and taxi operators if they had happened to notice an approximately ten-year-old boy in the company of a rather confused-looking elderly couple.

But neither Grandfather nor Miss Schneider appeared in the least bit confused. Both of them stared out of the window: Grandfather right into the heart of the beautiful green landscape; Miss Schneider longingly at

the blue sky overhead, as though she were still on the lookout for the sun, which was – for the moment – in the southeast, directly behind the bus as it drove on. Max knew that it would stay there a long time, as they were headed northwest to . . .

"To the summer meadow," said Grandfather after a pause.

"Yep," said Max.

"Where I kissed your grandmother for the first time. And asked her to be my wife."

"Yep."

From behind the front seat rose the chirping, bird-like voice of Miss Schneider. "I bet you're a good kisser."

"If I were to kiss you," Grandfather replied, "you would hear the angels sing!"

Miss Schneider started to laugh – *a young girl's laugh, clear as a bell,* Max thought – but she was cut off when a gong sounded, and a friendly-but-bored man's voice announced the next stop.

"Blossom Valley."

They got off the bus slowly – taking all the time in the world – then walked on, leaving the bus stop behind them. The street came to an end and a country lane began. Now the sun was shining on them, and every step carried them deeper and deeper into the summer-hazy, color-spangled green glow. They walked unhurriedly at a pace that seemed a little too slow, until, at some point, Miss Schneider began to scurry on ahead – at first slowly, then faster and faster, like an animal that has escaped from its cage and only now realizes that there are no more walls curbing its freedom.

(12)   *A Summer Day - Evening (Prokofiev)*

There are magical places in the world – children know this, and some grown-ups know it too – places where enchantment is at work. Places that radiate a power, even at a distance, that reaches deep into our human thoughts and feelings. For some, it is a small, hidden lake, far out in the wilderness, a deep-blue lake in which all of the clouds in the sky are reflected. Others may find such a place in the middle of a bustling city where – on a busy boulevard – a lone flower holds its ground against exhaust fumes of the countless cars zooming around it. And for others still, it is the silence of the inside of a church.

The large meadow that lay nestled on the slope of Blossom Valley was beautiful, to be sure – but that

wasn't what made it special. Beetles clambered along leaves and wildflowers, butterflies teetered drunkenly through the lush, sweet, windswept air – but even that wasn't what made it special. The special thing happened when you let yourself sink slowly into the tall grass and pressed your hands into earth, which was firm and yet soft too, as though it could breathe. You closed your eyes, you breathed deeply in and out, and in no time at all you felt rooted and alive. Your thoughts became clear and orderly: the right thoughts flowed through your mind like cool, wet silver, and the wrong thoughts burned up like rust in a very hot fire.

That was what the meadow in Blossom Valley was like. In such meadows, people kiss each other – or even make marriage proposals. You yourself pull a little box from your pocket and proudly show off the first tooth you've lost. Or, without being ashamed, you tell about getting a D on your math test. Or you excitedly report that you managed to watch *The Wizard of Oz* all the way through for the first time, without looking away when the flying monkeys tore apart the scarecrow. And while you tell these and other stories, summer after summer, year after year, your small, young hands are resting in larger, older ones. And when you fall silent, your eyes trace

the veins and sinews of the blotchy hands that have watched over, protected, and comforted you summer after summer, year after year – for as long as you can remember.

Max looked away from Grandfather's hands and gazed down into the meadow. He saw the stony path where Miss Schneider was still scurrying back and forth dreamily, as if she was measuring out an invisible room for herself; beyond, the brook that bubbled almost soundlessly along the path; past the brook, more meadow; and finally, the forest. And above that . . .

"Look," said Max. The moon had risen above the forest – milky-white in the blue sky, a quarter-moon that bulged out on the left side. "Why can you see it during the day on some days but not on others?"

"That depends on its position relative to both the sun and the earth," said Grandfather. "At the moment it's waning – in about a week it will be a new moon, and then we won't be able to see it at all, even though it's right up there above us."

"Why not?"

"Because the sun will be shining on it from behind."

"So it's still there, just not visible to us?"

"Exactly."

Max thought this over. He knew that the moon revolved around the earth, the earth around itself and – together *with* the moon orbiting it – around the sun too, and not in a single plane but in differently angled orbits. He began to feel dizzy.

"That's a heck of a lot of spinning," he said quietly.

Grandfather sniffled. "What?"

"All that about the moon."

"About the . . . " His grandfather raised his arm, stretched out his finger, and then let it sink again. He stared at Max, wrinkling his brow. "Who are you?"

(14)   A Summer Day – The Moon above the Meadow (Prokofiev)

To keep the Great Forgetting away from Grandfather when it tried to grab hold of him, it was sometimes enough to hug him tightly, offering nearness and security. For three minutes, then four, they sat in a silent embrace, until Grandfather cleared his throat and said, as if nothing had happened: "Your mother will be worried when she finds out you've been kidnapping old people instead of going to school."

Max breathed a sigh of relief. This was a difficult subject, but not nearly as difficult as the Great Forgetting. "She wouldn't have let me come by myself to go on a walk with you. Nobody would have let me come!"

He heard himself speaking and wished that his voice didn't sound so defiant.

"I'm thirsty," said Grandfather.

There were juice boxes in the backpack, along with some cookies and a few chocolate bars. Grandfather gratefully took a sip, and then gestured toward the stony path. He grinned.

"Well, take a look at that kooky Schneider! She's finally lost the last of her marbles!"

Max had never really let Miss Schneider out of his sight, but hadn't been paying close attention either, as sometimes happens when your gaze is fixed on something while your mind is off somewhere else. Now he focused on her. She wasn't scurrying about anymore. Instead, she stretched both of her arms sideways from her angular body as though she wanted to fly away – to the sun, if she could – then raised them upward as if she were going to fold them over her head. Then she brought her left leg forward and stepped with her right one to the side.

"Is she trying to dance?" Max asked in a low voice.

Miss Schneider seemed to buckle like a blade of grass buffeted by a sudden gust of wind, but she caught herself at once.

"Hasn't practiced in a while," said Grandfather, as the dancer, unfazed, brought herself once more into position. But as her performance continued, he became more and more attentive, began to smile, and from time to time said things like: "Now she's overdoing it!" or: "Don't you think she's . . . *trumpeting* about a bit too much?"

(16)   Petite Suite – Trumpet and Drum. Marche (Bizet)

Max thought she was wonderful. Watching Miss Schneider dance was like watching the sun spill itself over the earth. Stiff arms and legs, now in motion, suddenly seemed touched by eternal youth, and from their graceful movements a lightness flowed throughout the valley: the yellow of the buttercups turned to gold, and the clover and grass shone greener beneath the light summoned by Miss Schneider's dancing. Her movements grew ever wilder as she twirled, marched, stamped, threw back her head, and spun with flailing arms; and from her lips a bubbling, joyous laugh escaped into the glimmering air.

It finally dawned on Max: she had been a dance instructor.

Now she danced to the sun.

(18) Petite Suite – Trumpet and Drum. Marche (Bizet)

The sun dance cost Max a box of limeade, which Miss
Schneider emptied in a single, elegant sip without
sitting down. She then stretched out on her back
a few yards away and began – and this was rather
strange – moving her arms and legs like she was doing
jumping jacks, clip-clap, clip-clap.

"Good gracious, Schneider, it's summer!" called
Grandfather in her direction. "Wrong time of year for
snow angels!"

Miss Schneider chirped something in reply, but a
sudden gust ran away with whatever it was. This didn't
seem to bother her, though, for she folded her hands
together behind her neck and gazed wide-eyed into the

sky, where a bank of clouds had just covered the sun. In a single moment, the splendor of the dance had faded. The air grew darker.

"I'm afraid," said Max.

"Afraid of what?"

"That someday I'll ask, *do you remember?*, and you won't remember anymore. And that someday . . . someday you will forget how much you love me."

"Max." The familiar hand lay on his shoulder. A gentle touch. "Don't be afraid. You don't need to be afraid of anything, my boy." The other hand pointed up beyond the trees and toward the pale, misty moon. "You can't always see the moon, but you know it's always there. Right?"

Max nodded.

"Good. Then that's all you need to know. That's really all you need to know. OK?"

And Max nodded once more. I wish I could tell you that right at that moment the sun burst through the clouds once more, but it didn't.

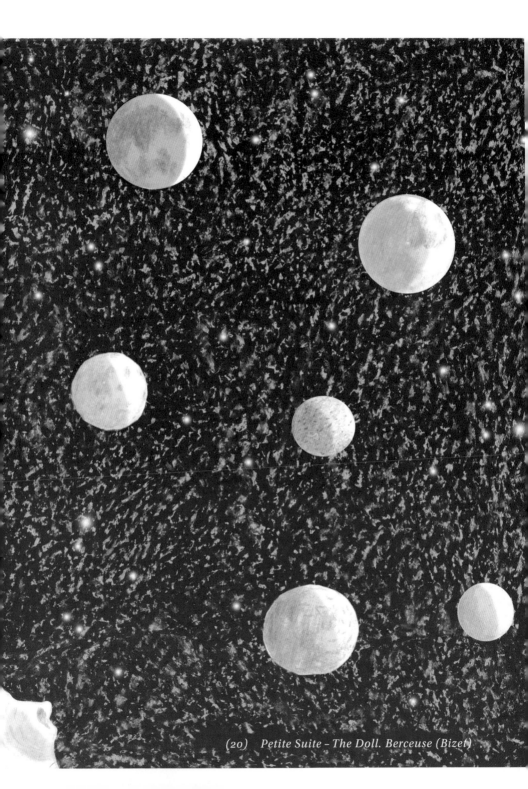

(20)   *Petite Suite – The Doll. Berceuse (Bizet)*

When they finally arrived – because of course they eventually did come: two caregivers, a few police officers, and Mama, who somehow managed to appear furious and relieved at the same time – when they arrived, everything happened so fast. Max immediately took off running, because in the movies the criminals usually run away when the police show up. His grandfather followed him, because good grandparents don't just let their grandchildren run away. Miss Schneider . . . well, it's hard to say, but we may just as well assume that she started running because everyone else was running too.

(22) *Petite Suite – The Top. Impromptu (Bizet)*

Grandfather had only made it fifty yards or so before his heart and lungs stopped cooperating. He paused, gasping for air, one hand pressed to his side, his face crimson but wearing a grin as wide as Niagara Falls.

Miss Schneider made it more than twice that distance and, who knows, might have made it all the way to the ocean – perhaps even over the first few yards of water; after all, she was as light as a feather – if she hadn't suddenly stopped and thrown herself behind a tussock of grass. This particular tussock was only about a foot high – not even tall enough for a raccoon to hide behind.

"To the sun!" rang out Miss Schneider's bird-like voice, as her pursuers gently took hold of her. Her battle

cry gave way to yelps of pain from one of the police officers, whom she had just kicked in the shin.

Only Max kept running, but when he glanced back
and realized that his flight was useless, he turned
around and darted back, right into the arms of his
mother – who had, very wisely, remembered Grandfather's fondness for the meadow in Blossom Valley.
Exhausted, Max pressed his face into her stomach. He
felt like crying, but he didn't. *Tired,* he thought, *I am so
tired, tired . . .*

When he felt something warm on his neck, he wasn't
sure if it was his mother's hand, or his grandfather's, or a
ray of sunlight.

(24)   *Petite Suite – Playing House. Duo (Bizet)*

Chiding from the caregivers (the door code was
changed), admonitions from the police, his mother's
sympathetic but disappointed face. . . . Even so, thought
Max as he lay in bed that night and mentally replayed
the day's events, even so, it hadn't been that bad when
they said goodbye to Grandfather and Miss Schneider
at the nursing home. All three of them had acted as if
they really had just been taking a walk – a pleasant stroll
with an impromptu dance thrown in as a bonus. Just as
he and his mother were leaving the common room, Miss
Schneider had whispered something in Grandfather's
ear and he had laughed – no doubt she wanted him to
kiss her so that she could hear the angels sing.

Max switched on his reading lamp, kicked off his summer bedspread, and got up. Right in front of the bed, he stood very straight and positioned himself. He breathed in, then out again. Lifted up his arms until his hands nearly touched above his head. Stepped forward with his left foot, stepped out to the side with his right, once more forward, once more sideways . . . and before he knew it, his feet had transported him out of the house and into the garden. Cool grass tickled him between his toes. He raised his head and turned slowly on the spot, as the earth revolves slowly on its axis. His eyes searched the sky. When, after five minutes, he still hadn't found the moon – but stars, countless silvery stars! – he went back inside and got into bed, comforted. He fell asleep instantly and dreamed that he laughed and ran, sprinting over the meadow in Blossom Valley – as fast as the wind – beyond the hills and toward the clear, blue horizon.

(26)   *Petite Suite – The Ball. Galop (Bizet)*

CD Contents

1   This Is the Story of Max

2   *A Summer Day – Morning (Prokofiev)*

3   Barely a Week Past His Birthday

4   *A Summer Day – Baseball (Prokofiev)*

5   In the Nursing Home

6   *A Summer Day – Waltz (Prokofiev)*

7   Is the Sun Shining Out There?

8   *A Summer Day – Regret (Prokofiev)*

9   The Code

10   *A Summer Day – March (Prokofiev)*

11   The Escape

12   *A Summer Day – Evening (Prokofiev)*

13   Magical Places

14   *A Summer Day – The Moon above the Meadow (Prokofiev)*

15   Preventing the Great Forgetting

16   *Petite Suite – Trumpet and Drum. Marche (Bizet)*

17   Miss Schneider

18   *Petite Suite – Trumpet and Drum. Marche (Bizet)*

19   Moon and Sun

20   *Petite Suite – The Doll. Berceuse (Bizet)*

21   Everyone Runs

22   *Petite Suite – The Top. Impromptu (Bizet)*

23   To the Sun

24   *Petite Suite – Playing House. Duo (Bizet)*

25   Countless Silvery Stars

26   *Petite Suite – The Ball. Galop (Bizet)*

69

Author	Andreas Steinhöfel
Narrator	Brett Barry
Music	Sergei Prokofiev: *A Summer Day*, op. 65a
	© Hawkes & Son (London) Ltd.
	Georges Bizet: *Jeux d'enfants (Children's Games)*, op. 22
	© G. Ricordi & Co., Bühnen- und Musikverlag GmbH
Conductor	Nicholas Simon
Orchestra	SWR Sinfonieorchester Baden-Baden und Freiburg
Recording Engineer	Bernhard Mangold-Märkel
Sound Engineer	Wolfgang Rein

The story was developed on behalf of SWR Sinfonieorchester Baden-Baden und Freiburg, in cooperation with the Ohrenspitzer project, for the children's concerts at the Freiburg Concert Hall and the Karlsruhe Concert Hall in November 2013.

© Dirk Steinhöfel

Andreas Steinhöfel is an award-winning German writer of children's books. He received the Erich Kästner Prize for Literature in 2009 and the German Children's Literature Award in 2013. In addition to writing books for young readers, he also works as a translator, writes for television and radio, and edits graphic novels. Born in 1962 in Battenberg, Germany, he now lives in Berlin. Other books by Andreas Steinhöfel available in English are *The Spaghetti Detectives, An Elk Dropped In,* and *At the Center of the World.*

Nele Palmtag, born in Böblingen, Germany, in 1973, began a career as a state-certified occupational therapist before studying design, fashion, and illustration at the University of the Arts Bremen and at Hamburg University of Applied Sciences. She illustrates her own

© Daniel Münter

picture books as well as those of other authors. Her own works have been translated into several languages. She lives with her family in Hamburg-Altona.

After completing *If My Moon Was Your Sun,* Andreas Steinhöfel and
Nele Palmtag met to discuss the genesis and development of the book.
We have summarized their comments below.

Andreas and Nele, how did you come up with Max?

Andreas Steinhöfel: I can still remember the first image that went
through my head. It always starts with an image. Over on one side
was a forest with a huge moon behind it, and on the other these little
people running around. And it was this little boy I thought of first:
a little boy named Max who is running after his grandpa, and who
is being followed in turn by this goofy Ms. Schneider. And then you
realize: yeah, I think I can make something out of that.

Nele Palmtag: I always find it easier developing the background
figures than the main characters. I always find them to be the most
difficult – they have to do so much.

  After that it's a bit like casting. The basic figure emerges from a
feeling, but then I draw fifty heads for Max and decide on one – or at
least on a general direction – and then keep developing them. First
he's too old or too young, too fat or too skinny – whatever it is. And I
think the fact that you always know someone who reminds you of the
character always plays into it, perhaps subconsciously. They always
seem familiar to me.

How did the music influence your writing and illustration?

Andreas Steinhöfel: I listened to the music for months on end, and
thought to myself: you have to find a narrative for the feeling that

this music awakens in you, one that communicates this emotion to the reader.

Nele Palmtag: I listened to the music and audio narration frequently until I had gotten a sense for myself of who this story is really about. And what I found so incredible was the impression that Andreas and the composer must have sat down together at some point, because everything flows together. I felt that the story is told to the tune of the music, so that the music can take over and continue telling it.

Andreas Steinhöfel: Which is great by the way, as music always brings this two-sided image with it.

Nele Palmtag: My first thought was: man, the music takes up an incredible amount of space. Someone might leaf through the book while listening to the CD, and the images should tell their own story during that time. Of course, the illustrations don't always recreate the same emotions that I felt: I wanted to stay within the flow of the narrative to answer the question: what happens next?

Andreas, how do you come up with your stories?

Andreas Steinhöfel: I always compare it to a cold glass of lemonade on a summer's day. You're sitting outside and, at some point, a layer of condensation forms on the glass. That's how it is with an image or an idea. After that moment when it first appears, my whole life begins circling this image. And everything that I experience or think of condenses onto this glass. Everything is then scrutinized according to the question: does it fit into the story or not? This drives the people around me crazy. It's always: oh, Andreas is writing a book (again). But that's just how it is. And it works, thank God, all by itself.

And I always come up with the conclusion first. For me, the conclusion is the light at the end of the tunnel. And then I simply start running towards it. And I might take a thousand detours, and perhaps once I'm finished the light at the end isn't even in the same tunnel, but at least I had an orientation. That's how it feels when writing and it was the same here. But in this case the feeling, called forth by the music, was new. I didn't have a textual idea, I had more of a musical feeling.

Nele, how do you create characters and images?

Nele Palmtag: When I develop characters, I have to establish a biography for each one. So I concern myself with, for example, how the grandfather lived. *What does his room look like? What are the characters wearing?* And maybe even something like, *what is his taste in music?* And so on.

Generally, I find it easier to illustrate stories that provide fewer images of their own. It was clear to me in this case that I needed to make a stronger effort to *interpret* the story. For example, Max wakes up in the morning, decides to go, and packs his things. We have no idea yet where this is going to go next. And so I thought: okay, we need a specific context where he is situated. And I don't want to show him sitting in bed or getting dressed. I don't want to portray things that are going to happen anyway. Instead I would like to find an image that puts the reader in the same mood that Max is in at the moment. He has to decide what to take on his picnic. And so that's how I arrived at the picture of the kitchen cupboard.

What is the title, If My Moon Was Your Sun, *all about?*

Andreas Steinhöfel: The title refers to the fact that Max's grandfather has dementia, and is slowly losing memory of his life. A black crow appears in nearly every illustration, which acts as a reminder that there is always something dark at work throughout the story – this threatening "Great Forgetting," as Max calls it, or perhaps, too, the real loss of his grandfather looming in the future.

And how do Max and his grandfather deal with this? That is the heart of the story. What happens when light trades places with darkness?

Good stories and good illustrations have a certain depth, and it is this depth that draws us to them. It's not for nothing that we often say that readers "lose themselves" in stories. They have a sort of irresistible attraction. And I hope that we've both achieved that here.